THE MURDERS IN THE RUE MORGUE

EDGAR ALLAN POE

REAL READS

www.realreads.co.uk

Retold by Gill Tavner
Illustrated by Felix Bennett

Published by Real Reads Ltd
Stroud, Gloucestershire, UK
www.realreads.co.uk

ISBN 978-1-906230-48-7

Printed in Singapore by Imago Ltd
Designed by Lucy Guenot
Typeset by Bookcraft Ltd, Stroud, Gloucestershire

CONTENTS

THE CHARACTERS

Monsieur Auguste Dupin

Intrigued by two recent murders, this young man attempts to use his sharp analytical skills to discover what happened in the Rue Morgue.

The narrator

He is keen to set you a challenge, and invites you to pit *your* analytical skills against those of his friend, Dupin.

You — the reader

How strong are your powers of analysis? Can you read minds? Can you beat Dupin to an explanation of the gruesome events in the Rue Morgue?

The murderer

Two brutal murders for which there is no apparent motive. Escape when there is no means of escape. The murderer has the police confounded.

A sailor

Why is he so anxious when he visits Dupin's apartment?

THE MURDERS IN THE RUE MORGUE

The world's most puzzling mysteries – what song the Syrens sang, for example, or what name Achilles assumed when he hid himself among women – can still be guessed at. They may even yet be solved.

Do you enjoy solving puzzles? Do you like crosswords, sudoku and logic puzzles? How about a game of chess or draughts? Maybe you enjoy working out 'whodunnit' in thrillers or detective stories before anyone else can.

If it's not something that you particularly enjoy, perhaps you know somebody who does. You may even know somebody who is extremely good at these sorts of things.

Quite often it seems to the rest of us that a person who is unusually good at puzzles, or is a good detective, is gifted with a sixth sense.

It seems as though they can just 'feel' the solution, as though they are 'inspired'. We can imagine that their mind works a bit like this:

MYSTERIOUS INSPIRATION

PROBLEM

SOLUTION

However, recent experiences are leading me to believe that this is not the case. In fact, quite contradicting the theory of 'inspiration', I would now argue that the minds of such people depend more upon logic than upon inspiration, like this:

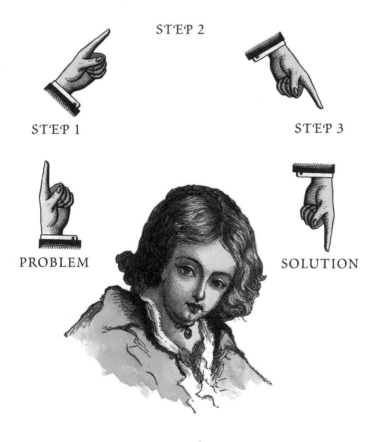

STEP 2

STEP 1

STEP 3

PROBLEM

SOLUTION

Far from relying upon inspiration in working out puzzles, it seems that a skilful person works very methodically, progressing carefully, step by step, towards a conclusion. Do you agree with me? This method is called *analysis*. A person who excels in this is considered to have an *analytical mind*.

This process can be illustrated in the way many computer games work, where you have to gather equipment or information in order to work systematically towards a goal or destination. Consider the goal as the solution to the mystery, the equipment or information as the logical steps necessary to get there.

An analytical person enjoys the mental exercise of working things out as much as an athletic person enjoys the physical challenge of working out in a gym. Is this how you see things too? Do *you* enjoy working out difficult puzzles? Are *you* analytical?

Here is a test or, if you prefer, a puzzle for you to work out, and I have to admit that it defeated me at the time. It is a faithful account of two most gruesome murders, in seemingly impossible circumstances. Can *you* work out what actually happened in the early hours of one fateful morning in the Rue Morgue?

Before you start, here are a few tips. To be a good detective you need the same skills as a good card-player. You must consider and examine *every detail*, not just the obvious ones. You have to observe every change in a person's face, everything they say, everything they do. You must always expect the unexpected. And you must remember it all.

In this most strange tale, you'll see an analytical friend of mine at work as he progresses step by step towards a conclusion. Can you make faster progress than he was able to? Can you beat him to the solution of the mystery? I will present the evidence in the order in which we received it ourselves.

Some years ago I was living in Paris. At that time Paris was an ideal city in which to spend time observing the world and reading to one's heart's content, both of which I love to do.

I had the good fortune of meeting a gentleman called Monsieur Auguste Dupin. We met by chance in the library, where we were both searching for the same book. We started chatting, went for a coffee, and over time became great friends.

Poor Dupin seemed tired and sad. He told me that he came from a wealthy family, but a series of unfortunate events had led to the loss of most of his money. In spite of his sadness, he retained a lively mind and a fresh, vivid imagination. He was just the kind of friend I needed at that point in my life.

Renting an apartment together, we led a strange life. In the daytime, we shut the sunlight out and spent our time reading and talking by candlelight. When the real darkness of night-time fell we walked around Paris together, watching what people were doing and very often lost in our own thoughts.

You think this is odd? Is it so very different from sitting in the dark watching the television or going to the cinema?No, the way we chose to pass the time wasn't particularly odd, but this fact is – *Dupin could read my mind!*

As we walked through the quiet streets, he would from time to time break the silence with a low chuckle. When I looked to him for an explanation, he answered, 'I know what you're thinking about.' At such times he would have an expression of madness on his face, his body would become rigid, his eyes wild, and his voice tense and high-pitched.

The first few times he did this I was disbelieving and slightly uneasy. I would challenge him: 'So tell me then, what *am* I thinking?' Yet the more it happened, the more my disbelief was replaced by amazement, my unease by curiosity. He was always right. But how could he possibly read my mind?

Have you ever tried to follow your train of thoughts backwards to see what it was that made you think of something? For example, a person might accidentally bump into you in the street and you suddenly remember that you have a maths test on Monday. Where did that thought come from?

It might have followed a route like this:

But that's not really very likely. It's more likely to have been like this:

Thus, maybe in less than a second, your chain of thoughts has taken you from an unfortunate collision to Monday's maths test. Does that make sense to you?

This is how Dupin explained his ability to read my mind. He would notice an event and, watching me closely, use logic and his knowledge of my character to work out my train of thought. No sixth sense, no mystery, just very clever, methodical, *analytical* thinking.

Enough of maths tests. Here's *your* test, relating to a gruesome double murder which occurred during our time in Paris; two very strange murders with very few clues.

We first learned about the deaths of Madame and Mademoiselle L'Espanaye in our newspaper, the *Gazette des Tribunaux*. Remember that I have advised you to consider *every* detail.

Murders ir

The mutilated bodies of an elderly lady and her daughter have been discovered in their home in the Rue Morgue. Police are still interviewing witnesses, but at present have very few clues.

Horrific Shrieks

At 3am this morning, inhabitants of the Rue Morgue were disturbed by a succession of horrific shrieks. The shrieks came from an apartment shared by Madame L'Espanaye and her daughter Mademoiselle Camille L'Espanaye.

Arguing

It took eight neighbours and two policemen to break through the gate and access the main building. By the time they reached the door of the L'Espanaye apartment on the fourth floor, the shrieks had stopped, to be replaced by two male voices arguing. By the time the witnesses succeeded in breaking through the door, the room was silent and nobody was there.

A police spokesman told us that the room was in a wild disorder. The bed was broken, and money and valuable jewellery were scattered on the floor. Police found a razor, covered in blood. On the hearth they found two or three long thick tresses of grey human hair, which seemed to have been pulled out in handfuls from the roots.

Strangled

The body of the younger victim was eventually found up the chimney. She had been pushed up feet-first with great force. Her face was badly scratched, and dark bruises on her neck suggested that she had been strangled.

Fearfully Mutilated

The body of her elderly mother was found soon after, in the small paved yard to the rear of the building. Her head had been entirely severed from her body, which itself was fearfully mutilated.

Anyone who has information relating to these brutal murders should inform the Gendarmerie on Rue Montmartre. All assistance will be treated in the strictest confidence.

Dupin was extraordinarily interested in this case. I observed him with fascination. Just as when he reads my mind, his eyes shone wildly and his voice was tense. The following morning, he rushed out to buy an early edition of the *Gazette*.

His keen interest was rewarded. The police had taken the most unusual step of providing the newspaper with details of all the witness statements they had received. This suggested that, unable to reach any conclusions themselves, they were throwing the case open to the public. Dupin's eyes blazed. He thrust the *Gazette* into my hands.

When I read the statements I was completely bemused. I've tabulated the witnesses' reports below for you. Can *you* make any sense of them? Most witnesses described two voices they heard arguing when the screaming had stopped. I have called these Voice 1 and Voice 2.

	Witness	Nationality	Occupation
	Pauline Duborg	French	Laundress
	Isidore Muste	French	Policeman
	Henri Duval	French	Neighbour
	Herr Odenheimer	Dutch	Restaurant owner
	Jules Mignaud	French	Bank manager
	Adolphe le Bon	French	Bank clerk
	William Bird	English	Tailor
	Alfonzo Garcio	Spanish	Undertaker
	Alberto Montani	Italian	Sweet shop owner

Observations	Description of Voice 1	Description of Voice 2
The victims were wealthy. e witness never saw any visitors at their apartment.		
ped to break into the house. The ams seemed as though somebody in great pain. Loud voices seemed to be arguing.	Male, gruff, French. Said 'diable', 'sacre' and 'mon dieu'.	Shrill, could be male or female. Possibly speaking Spanish.
e victims had lived there for six ars and never had visitors. The dow shutters were always closed, pt at the window of the large back om on the fourth storey, where ess believes the ladies spent most heir time. Knew the victims well.	Male, gruff, French. Said 'diable', 'sacre' and 'mon dieu'.	Shrill, could be male or female. Definitely not the voice of either of the victims. Possibly speaking Italian.
ieks seemed to last ten minutes. red the house with the policemen.	Male, gruff, French. Said 'diable', 'sacre' and 'mon dieu'.	Harsh, frightened and angry. Loud and quick. Possibly speaking French.
e days before her death, Madame panaye took out 4,000 Francs in . The money was conveyed to her home by the bank's clerk.		
ree days before the murders he companied Mme L'Espanaye to home, with the gold in two bags. 't see anybody in the street. It is a very quiet back-street.		
ped to force entry into the house. d the sounds of people struggling – scraping and shuffling.	Gruff, a Frenchman. Heard distinctly 'sacre' and 'mon dieu'.	Possibly a woman. Louder than voice 1. Definitely not English – sounded German, although Bird himself does not speak German.
	Gruff. Frenchman.	Shrill. Englishman. Mr Garcio does not speak any English. He guessed from the intonation.
	Gruff. Frenchman.	Thinks it might be Russian.

The report included some further bewildering facts:

- The door of the room in which Mademoiselle L'Espanaye's body was found was locked from the inside.

- By the time the neighbours and policemen entered, the place was silent and empty.

- The windows of both the front and back rooms were closed and locked from the inside.

- A door between the two rooms was closed, but not locked.

- The door leading from the front room into the passage was locked, with the key on the inside.

- A small front room on the fourth storey was open and the door ajar. It was crowded with old furniture and boxes.

- The time between the arguing voices and the successful breaking down of the door was somewhere between three and five minutes.

- The chimneys were all too narrow for a human to pass down them.

- There is no rear entrance to the property.

- Mademoiselle L'Espanaye's body was so firmly wedged up the chimney that it took five men to pull her down.

- The money delivered by the bank clerk three days ago had not been taken. It was found on the floor in its original bags.

Dupin seemed extraordinarily interested in the affair. By good fortune, he was acquainted with the Prefect of the Police, through whom he soon succeeded in acquiring a copy of the physician's report on the two bodies.

Report on the bodies found in the case of the Rue Morgue Murders.

Name: Paul Dumas   Profession: Physician

Deceased: 1. Mme L'Espanaye 2. Mlle Camille L'Espanaye

Time of examination: 6 a.m.

Location of bodies: The residence of the deceased. Rue Morgue, Quartier St. Roch, Paris. Both bodies lying on the bed in the room in which Mlle L. was found.

Description of body 1: All bones of the right leg and arm are shattered. Ribs on the left side are splintered. Whole body, head and face bruised and discoloured. Head severed from body by a sharp instrument, possibly a razor.

Description of body 2: Bruised and badly grazed. Throat bruised — look like finger imprints. Several deep scratches below the chin. Tongue partially bitten through. Large bruise on stomach.

Additional information: Several thick tresses of human hair, clotted with flesh from the scalp, were found on the hearth. I confirm that this was the hair of Mme L'Espanaye.

Conclusions: Were the windows not securely closed from the inside, I would believe the broken bones due to a fall from the window. However, I must conclude that Mme L'Espanaye was beaten. The wounds could only have been inflicted by a person of great strength. Death was caused by the cutting of the throat.

Mlle L'Espanaye seems to have been throttled to death before being thrust feet-first up the chimney.

Signature: Paul Dumas

Later that same day, looking up from his eagerly-acquired evening edition of the *Gazette*, Dupin told me that Adolphe le Bon, the bank clerk, had been arrested, although there did not appear to be any incriminating evidence. 'What is your opinion of these murders?' he asked me.

I confessed that I was entirely baffled.

'The police are doing a poor job,' sighed Dupin, carefully folding the paper. 'There is no method in their proceedings.' I looked at him for further explanation. 'They are impairing their vision by holding the object too close.' He was now on his feet, heading towards the door. 'Let's go and see for ourselves.'

We arrived in the Rue Morgue late in the afternoon. Dupin's previously mentioned connection with the Prefect of Police meant that we had easily obtained permission to visit the premises. Before entering, we walked up the street, turned down an alley and round to the rear of the building. As we walked, Dupin examined the whole area with an attention to detail for which I could see no obvious reason. He remained silent.

Entering the building, we went straight upstairs to the room in which the bodies still lay. Dupin scrutinised everything, including the bodies, in such minute detail that it was dark by the time we left. All the way home, he declined to discuss the murders.

It wasn't until noon the next day, as we sat together at home, that he suddenly asked me, 'Did you observe anything *peculiar* yesterday?'

Something in the way he emphasised 'peculiar' made me shudder. I answered that I had seen nothing more than was reported in the *Gazette*.

'But the *Gazette* has not entered into the unusual horror of the murders. This horror, which so confounds the police, should make the case easy to solve. They are also puzzled by the different descriptions of the voices, and by the fact that nobody was discovered upstairs, even though there could have been no escape without passing those ascending the stairs. These factors should lead us towards a conclusion, not away from one. We should not ask "What has occurred?" but "What has occurred that has never occurred before?" This is what has led me to the solution of this mystery.'

The solution? I was astonished. How could these strange factors, so bewildering to me, already have led Dupin to a conclusion? If you remember what I told you earlier of his analytical skill, you may not be surprised by his progress. Maybe you have been able to find a solution as quickly as Dupin, but I expect you are as lost as I was.

I stared at my friend in mute astonishment.

'I am now awaiting somebody,' he said. I continued to stare. Dupin read the increased anxiety in my face. 'I am not awaiting the murderer himself,' he reassured me, 'but a person who must have been implicated in the events in the Rue Morgue. He may not arrive, but if he does it will be necessary to detain him.'

Dupin handed me one of two pistols, which I took eagerly. He then began to lead me, step by meticulously-detailed step, through

the process by which he had reached his
conclusion. To him, the workings of my own
mind must have seemed excessively laborious.
I wonder whether you will fare any better. You
have a slight advantage over me, as I have
placed Dupin's reasoning below in tabular
form, whereas I had to listen very carefully to
his complicated explanation.

Evidence

The two voices heard after the screams were definitely
not the voices of the deceased ladies.

When the witnesses broke in, the murderer(s)
were no longer there.

The doors were locked from the inside. The chimneys were t
narrow for a human body to get through. No secret exits we:
found. The windows appeared to be fastened shut.

If the murderer(s) had escaped via a door or a front window
they would have been seen by the crowd who had
rushed up the stairs.

The rear windows appeared to be
nailed shut from the inside.

Upon close examination, Dupin discovered that the nails we:
attached to concealed springs, which thrust them into the wo
when the sash windows slid into their closed positions.

If we accept that the window was open,
we must assume that Mme L'Espanaye's
body was thrown from it.

This small part of the mystery I acknowledged
solved. The murderer had entered and exited
via a window which had then slid closed, a
locking mechanism springing into place. But
the window in question was four storeys above

Conclusion

The murders were perpetrated by a third party – at least two others being involved.

They were not ghosts or spirits, so they must have found a physical means of escape.

These are the only escape options. Although escape seems impossible, it must somehow have been possible. Therefore, one of these must not be as it seems.

They escaped via a
rear window.

This must not be the case, as they are the only possible exit. The windows therefore have the power
of fastening themselves.

One of the windows must have slid closed,
and the nail sprung across to lock it
after the murderer(s) escaped.

Mme L'Espanaye's broken bones and bruises were
caused by the fall, not, as the physician concluded,
by a severe beating.

the ground. 'I see that your next question is that of the mode of ascent and descent,' Dupin read my mind. 'Upon this point I satisfied myself when we walked around the back of the building before we entered.'

Evidence	Conclusion
About 1.5 metres from the window in question there runs a lightning rod. The wooden shutters of the window are particularly wide. If swung fully back to the wall, one would reach to within about 75 centimetres of the lightning rod.	The murderer must have climbed the rod, grasped the lattice of the shutter and, pushing against the wall with his feet, swung the shutter closed and sprung himself through the window and into the room. He could have exited by the reverse of this procedure.
At the foot of the lightning rod, Dupin found a piece of ribbon tied in a knot so complicated that few besides sailors could have tied it.	As yet, no conclusion.

'I wish to impress upon you,' said Dupin, 'the almost superhuman strength and agility required to carry out this acrobatic feat. This is important. Remember – it is the strange things that happened in spite of their improbability which make this case so easy to solve.'

I don't know how you the reader are getting on, but I was not, at this point, finding it particularly easy.

Dupin now invited me to consider further the witness reports of the voices heard arguing in the apartment. 'The witnesses, you will have observed, were all in agreement about the gruff voice. They knew that it was French, and they could identify particular words.'

'Yes,' I acknowledged this to be true, 'but there was much disagreement in regard to the second, shrill voice.'

Evidence	Conclusion
Not only did the witnesses disagree on the language spoken by the second voice, but all of them identified the speaker as a foreigner. Amongst those witnesses, who between them represented most of the great languages of Europe, not one was able to identify the language as his own.	It could have been an Asian or an African language, or a less-well-known European language such as Estonian, Russian or Icelandic.
There are very few people in Paris who speak these less well known languages.	We might still consider this a possibility, but its improbability must also be allowed.
The voice was described by one witness as 'harsh rather than shrill,' and by two others as 'quick and unequal.' No individual words were distinguishable.	At this point, the strangeness of the voice must be accepted as a fact. It should therefore contribute to a conclusion.

Dupin summarised his conclusions so far. 'I wish you to bear in mind the evidence we now have of the unusual degree of strength, agility and courage shown in entering and departing from the room, alongside the strange nature of the voice.' This gave me a vague, half-formed idea. I was on the verge of understanding without being able to understand. It felt the same as those occasions when you are on the brink of remembering something, like a person's name for example, but just cannot grasp the memory.

Dupin then began to explain the further conclusions he had been able to draw from the appearance of the rooms when we arrived.

Evidence	Conclusion
The drawers of the bureau had been rifled, but it seemed that nothing had been taken. The four thousand francs in gold, brought by the bank clerk three days earlier, was discovered in its original bags on the floor.	If theft had been the motive, only an idiot would have abandoned both the gold and the motive. The fact that the gold was delivered three days before the murders is merely coincidence. We are therefore without a motive.
The murders were atrocious and unusual. One body was thrust feet-first up a chimney. Mme L'Espanaye's head was completely severed from its body by a mere razor, and a whole fistful of hair, and its roots, had been pulled from her head.	What murderer could be so strong, or so depraved? For such unusual murders, an unusual answer must be sought.

'What impression has this made upon you?'
Dupin asked me.

My flesh creeping, I replied, 'I can only
think that a madman, or some raving maniac
escaped from a neighbouring asylum, could
have committed the murders.'

'Your idea is not irrelevant,' said Dupin,
'but now take a look at this.' He held out a tuft
of coarse, tawny-coloured hair. 'I disentangled
this from the rigidly clenched fingers of Mme
L'Espanaye.'

It was not human hair.

Dupin then showed me some measurements he had taken of the bruises on Mlle L'Espanaye's neck, and invited me to measure my own hand against them. I made the attempt in vain. The marks were too far apart. 'This,' I said, 'is the mark of no human hand.'

'Now read this,' said Dupin, passing me
a book by Cuvier, a famous French zoologist.
It was open on a page describing the orang-
utan of the East Indies: a strong and ferocious
creature. I understood the full horrors of the
murders at once. I imagine that you have too.

The murders themselves might now have been
solved, but I was still puzzled by the accounts
of the two voices. Dupin explained further.
'A Frenchman was witness to, or arrived just
after the murders. His exclamation of "Mon
dieu" was one of horror. It is only a guess, but
it is likely that the creature had escaped from
the Frenchman's care prior to committing
the murders.' He then handed me a copy of
a newspaper called *Le Monde*, popular with
sailors. 'I have placed an advertisement in the
paper. It should bring the Frenchman to our
residence,' he said.

Remembering the pistol in my hand, I laid it on the table, took the paper and read Dupin's advertisement.

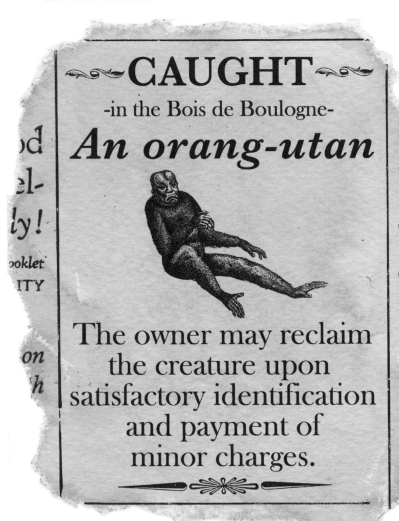

~~CAUGHT~~

-in the Bois de Boulogne-

An orang-utan

The owner may reclaim the creature upon satisfactory identification and payment of minor charges.

It then gave our address.

'I am not sure that this will work,' admitted Dupin, 'but the knotted ribbon I found suggests that the Frenchman in question was a sailor, who had captured the beast on one of his voyages, in the hope of profiting from his sale. I have said that the creature was found in the Bois de Boulogne, a long way from here, so that the sailor will not believe his beast to be suspected of the murders. He is therefore more likely to come to collect him.'

At that moment we heard a footstep outside, followed by a rapping at the door. I picked up my pistol and hid it behind my back.

'Come in,' said Dupin, in a cheerful tone.

A tall, muscular man entered. His sunburnt face, half-hidden by beard and moustache, confirmed him as a sailor. He bowed awkwardly and bade us good evening in an accent which confirmed him as a native Frenchman.

'Sit down, my friend,' said Dupin. 'Your orang-utan is a remarkably fine creature and no doubt very valuable.'

'Have you got him here?' asked the Frenchman, looking nervously around. 'I am very willing to pay you a reward for finding him.'

'Well,' replied Dupin. 'Let me think – what reward should I have? Oh! I know! As my reward you shall tell me everything you know about the murders in the Rue Morgue.'

The sailor flushed and started to his feet, before falling back into his chair, trembling violently. I pitied him from the bottom of my heart.

'My friend,' said Dupin in a kind tone, 'I pledge you the honour of a gentleman that we intend you no injury. You are not guilty of the murders, but you are bound by every principle of honour to reveal all that you know. An innocent man is now imprisoned, charged with this crime.'

I remembered the unfortunate bank clerk.

'So help me God,' said the sailor, recovering his presence of mind. 'I *am* innocent, and I *will* tell you all that I know.'

Your analytical faculties having been exercised by this story, and your desire to hear the concluding pieces of evidence being probably strong, I will present to you the sailor's story in linear form. This seems most suitable for our present state of mind.

He captured the orang-utan in Borneo. He brought it home and kept it secretly in his home in Paris, until such a time as he could sell it. He came home one evening to find that the creature had escaped from its bonds and, its face covered in shaving foam, was trying to imitate the action of shaving, razor in hand. The sailor seized his whip in an attempt to capture the creature. Terrified, and still clutching the razor, the creature fled into the open street. The sailor gave chase.

The creature ran into the Rue Morgue, where its attention was caught by a light gleaming from an open window on the fourth floor. It climbed into the window as surmised by Dupin. The sailor easily climbed the lightning rod, but was unable to swing on the shutter. All that he could do was reach over far enough to catch a glimpse of the room's interior. He was horrified by what he saw.

The screams of the two ladies turned the creature from peaceful and curious to terrified and angry. The more it attacked, the more the ladies screamed, and the more frenzied it became. When the ladies were dead, it seemed conscious of having done wrong. To conceal its crimes, it thrust the younger lady up the chimney and flung the elder from the window. At this point the sailor fled, abandoning in his terror all concern for the beast.

There is little more to add. The orang-utan must have escaped from the room as Dupin described. The sailor eventually captured his creature, and sold him for a very large sum. The bank clerk was released from prison. The Prefect of Police could not conceal his displeasure that Dupin had solved the mystery where he himself had so completely failed. 'People really ought to mind their own business,' he complained bitterly.

'Let him complain,' said Dupin. 'It will ease his conscience. In truth, it is no surprise that he failed in the solution of this mystery, for he is somewhat too cunning to be profound. His wisdom is all head and no body, for he seeks to ignore that which is, and to explain that which is not.'

And so, I return my attention to you, the reader. You will acknowledge that Dupin succeeded because he paid close attention to every piece of evidence, accepting it as fact and working from there, just as when he read my mind. This is how an analytical mind works.

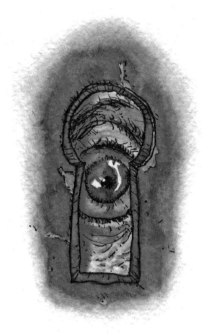

How close did you come to solving the murders in the Rue Morgue? Were you ever a step ahead of Dupin? Somehow I suspect not, unless you too are an analytic genius.

TAKING THINGS FURTHER

The real read

This *Real Reads* version of *The Murders in the Rue Morgue* is a retelling of Edgar Allan Poe's chilling short story, which is one of his *Tales of Mystery and Imagination*. If you would like to read the story in all its original complexity and horror, alongside Poe's other short stories, many complete editions of his *Tales of Mystery and Imagination* are available, from bargain paperbacks to beautifully-bound hardbacks. You may well find a copy in your local library.

Filling in the spaces

The loss of so many of Edgar Allan Poe's original words is a sad but necessary part of the shortening process. Although we haven't had to omit subplots, we have had to reduce the complexity of Poe's language and the detail of his discursive and descriptive style, both of which are a loss. The points below will help to give you an even greater sense of the original, and may give you the confidence to read it yourself.

● Poe's *The Murders in the Rue Morgue* is written entirely in prose. The direct challenge to the reader and the presentation of material in the form of tables, are features of this *Real Reads* version, not of the original.

● The narrator of *The Murders in the Rue Morgue* does address the reader, although less directly than in this *Real Reads* version, referring to the reader as 'the reader'.

● References to such relatively modern pastimes as crosswords and sudoku are, of course, not present in the original. Poe does, however, discuss chess, draughts and card games. For an example of his style, read the following paragraph, in which he compares chess and draughts: 'I will therefore take occasion to assert that the higher powers of the reflective intellect are more decidedly and more usefully tasked by the unostentatious game of draughts than by all the elaborate frivolity of chess.'

● For a further taste of Poe's style, read the paragraph below which is the introduction to Inspector Dupin. You can compare this with the same passage in the *Real Reads* version: 'This young gentleman was of an excellent – indeed of an illustrious family, but, by a variety of untoward events, had been reduced to such poverty that the energy of his character succumbed beneath it, and he ceased to bestir himself in the world, or to care for the retrieval of his fortunes.'

● In Poe's day relatively little was known about 'wild beasts'. His assumptions about the likely behaviour of an orang utan reflect the limited knowledge of his time.

Back in time

Edgar Poe was born in Boston, Massachusetts, USA in 1809. Orphaned at an early age, he was cared for by John and Frances Allan of Richmond, Virginia, hence the addition of Allan to his name. He spent some of his childhood in England, returning to the USA in 1820.

His early adulthood was rather unsettled, with erratic relations with the Allans. His attempts to settle into army life ended when he deliberately ensured his own court-martial. In his twenties he married his thirteen-year-old cousin. The cause of Poe's death, at the age of only forty, is not known. It is possible that he was a victim of cooping – a brutal kidnapping and drugging by which people were forced to vote a particular way in elections. However, this is not certain, and other causes such as tuberculosis or a brain haemorrhage are also possible.

As a writer, Poe is now best known for his *Tales of Mystery and Imagination*, of which *The Murders in the Rue Morgue* is one of the more famous. However, most of his life he earned money as a literary critic and assistant editor of periodicals. Although already a prolific writer of poetry and prose, it wasn't until the publication in 1845 of his poem *The Raven* that he became a household name.

Poe is considered to be the originator of the detective genre of fiction, with *The Murders in the Rue Morgue* being the first example. The word 'detective' didn't even exist in the English language at the time. Arthur Conan Doyle, the creator of Sherlock Holmes, once asked, rhetorically, 'Where was the detective story until

Poe breathed the breath of life into it?' Sherlock Holmes' methods of deduction are clearly influenced by those of Monsieur Auguste Dupin. After his introduction in *The Murders in the Rue Morgue*, Dupin also features in Poe's *The Mystery of Marie Roget* and *The Purloined Letter*.

The analytical process in which Dupin works can be seen as evidence of Poe's rejection of transcendentalism, a popular philosophy in the USA at the time. Transcendentalism valued intuition and spirituality above the physical and empirical. The extract below, taken from Poe's description of an analytical man early in *The Murders in the Rue Morgue*, argues his case: 'He is fond of enigmas, of conundrums, of hieroglyphics; exhibiting in his solutions of each a degree of acumen which appears to the ordinary apprehension preternatural. His results, brought about by the very soul and essence of method, have, in truth, the whole air of intuition.'

He is arguing that real analytical skill can often seem almost supernatural, although it is completely the opposite. In spite of this, Poe's use of dark, gothic settings seems to draw upon the romantic movement in the UK at the time, which valued the power of imagination and inspiration highly.

Poe is also considered to have greatly influenced the genres of both horror and science fiction, as well as being the first writer to establish the requirements of an effective short story. He is regarded as one of America's most important writers, helping them to move out of the shadow of English writers.

Finding out more

We recommend the following books and websites to gain a greater understanding of Edgar Allan Poe and the world he lived in.

Books

There are many collections of Poe's short stories, poems and essays; far too many to select any for this list. Just ask in a library or bookshop.

● *The Graphic Classics Series* has a volume devoted to Poe. Volume 1: *Edgar Allan Poe*, Eureka Productions, 2006.

- J. Patrick Lewis and Michael Slack, *Poe's Pie: Maths Puzzlers in Classic Poems*, Harcourt Children's Books, 2012.

Websites

- www.poemuseum.org
The Poe Museum is in Richmond, Virginia, where Poe spent many years. This excellent website has details of Poe's life work, and there is a helpful section for teachers through which they can request a classroom activity pack.

- http://www.eapoe.org/
The site of the Edgar Allan Poe Society of Baltimore. Interesting information, and very up to date.

Film

The following five film titles were directed by Roger Corman in the 1960s, and are produced by Twentieth Century Fox (note that they are rated 15):

- The Raven
- The Pit and the Pendulum

- Masque of the Red Death
- Fall of the House of Usher
- House of Wax

Whilst there are films entitled 'The Murders in the Rue Morgue', we cannot find an accurate adaptation of Poe's story.

Food for thought

Here are some things to think about if you are reading *The Murders in the Rue Morgue* alone, or ideas for discussion if you are reading it with friends. In retelling *The Murders in the Rue Morgue* we have tried to recreate, as accurately as possible, Poe's original plot and characters. We have also tried to imitate aspects of his style. Remember, however, that this is not the original work; thinking about the points below, therefore, can only help you begin to understand Poe's craft. To move forward from here, turn to the full-length version of *The Murders in the Rue Morgue* and experience his distinctive style of writing.

Starting points

- Does the narrator succeed in making you want to solve the mystery?

- What interests you about the character of Dupin?

- How helpful did you find the drawings on pages 8, 9, 15 and 16?

- How easily were you able to take in the details of all the witness statements?

- Were you ever ahead of Dupin?

- What horrified you most about the murders?

- What puzzled you most about the murders?

- What did you think when Dupin explained the murderer's identity?

- What do you think of the story's ending?

Themes

What do you think Edgar Allan Poe is saying about the following themes in *The Murders in the Rue Morgue*?

- logic and analysis
- inspiration and intuition
- brutality

Style

Here are some things to think about relating to Poe's style and the style of this *Real Reads* version of *The Murders in the Rue Morgue*:

- *Real Reads* decided to put some of the story in the form of pictures and tables. What did you think about these?

- What do you think about the way in which the narrator talks directly to you as the reader?

- Using *The Murders in the Rue Morgue* as a starting point, what would you list as features which distinguish a short story from a novel?

- Can you write a mystery for a reader to solve? In doing so, try to use some of these features of Poe's style.